Summer Pony

Summer Pony

JEAN SLAUGHTER DOTY

Illustrated by Sam Savitt

SCHOLASTIC INC.

NEW YORK · TORONTO · LONDON · AUCKLAND · SYDNEY · TOKYO

ISBN 0-590-09851-9

20 19 18 17 16 15 14 13 12 11 10   2 3 4 5 6 7/8

Printed in the U.S.A.   11

To my father—Charles E. Slaughter—
for the fence post holes he dug,
for the little red barn he built,
and especially for his many hours
of patience and understanding—
this book is affectionately and
gratefully dedicated.

Chapter One

It was a miserable gray day in March, with a threat of late snow in the air, when the station wagon bumped to a stop by the shabby barn.

Ginny was shivering as she got out of the car and waited for her mother. Somehow, everything here seemed unpleasant and unreal. This was the

1

day her dreams were supposed to come true. She was to have a pony, a pony of her own, for the whole summer ahead. Arrangements had already been made with the owner of the Sweetbriar Pony Farm for her to choose any one of all the ponies in his stable. But something was wrong. They must have made a wrong turn off the main road. Nobody could keep ponies in a place like this.

She could feel the cold mud oozing through her sneakers. Her mother came up beside her. She wore her let's-make-the-best-of-an-unpleasant-situation look on her face. "Here we are, dear. I wonder where Mr. Dobbs can be?"

The ponies of her dreams flashed through Ginny's mind. Which would she choose? A bright red-gold chestnut with a cream mane and tail? A black pony, with slim, elegant legs and a beautiful head like an Arabian? Or maybe a gray, the color of smoke? Shining coats and shining eyes, sleek and beautiful, waiting for her to choose— but not here. Certainly not here.

"Mother," Ginny whispered. "This can't be right. I never saw such an awful place." But Ginny knew, even as she stumbled after her mother, that this was, indeed, the Sweetbriar Pony Farm. A faded sign saying so hung on the side of the sagging barn, and three little ponies, with their backs humped up against the cold wind, stood in a nearby field behind a rusty wire fence. A wheelbarrow with a broken handle was tipped over next to a soggy pile of manure close to the barn and there were hoofprints everywhere in the mud around them.

A narrow door opened with a squeal of hinges and a tall, thin man came out. "Thought I heard a car," he said. "You must be Mrs. Anderson come to choose a pony for the summer. Morning, miss. You must be the lucky little girl."

He stood back and waved toward the darkness behind the open door. "Come in, come in and meet the ponies. Twenty of them, ma'am. All for you to choose from. Every one of them a pet, guaranteed sound as a bell, safe for any child to ride and drive."

"Yuk!" said Ginny under her breath as she followed her mother through the narrow door into the dimness of the long barn.

Some daylight managed to struggle through the dirty windows and two or three dim light

3

bulbs burned unenthusiastically down the aisle. Here were no shining ponies waiting for her, turning their elegant heads toward her as she came through the door. Instead, in long rows of narrow stalls, divided by broken boards held together with pieces of baling wire, stood odds and ends of ponies of all possible shapes and sizes, most of them very small and all of them thin and shabby.

"My daughter has not had much riding experience," Ginny heard her mother say. "Just a few years away at a camp where they taught riding once a week. But she has always dreamed of having a pony of her own, so instead of sending her back to camp, we thought a pony rented for the summer, to keep at home—as a birthday present . . ."

Mr. Dobbs mumbled an answer but Ginny didn't hear. She moved down the narrow aisle between the stalls, looking unbelievingly at the ponies on either side.

"You poor little things," Ginny whispered as the ponies turned their heads to watch her as she passed. The air was stale and sour and heavy, and smelled of dirty ponies and dirty stalls. Ginny

4

wanted to cry. She wanted to run outside, forget this awful place, and go and find the white-fenced pony farm which *must* exist somewhere and where her dream ponies must be waiting.

But she knew at the same time that only this was real. Arrangements had been made, her parents had said. Someone had recommended Mr. Dobbs—how could this be?—and so her mother and father, who knew nothing about horses and ponies, had somehow found the Sweetbriar Pony Farm. Her choice of pony was to be here. Or no pony . . . anywhere . . . at all.

Ginny took a long, shivery breath and went on down the aisle. Most of the ponies were little Shetlands, much too small to carry her, but she could make out a taller chestnut, with a white blaze on his face, that was big enough to carry her. She stopped hopefully near his stall, admiring the pony's beautiful head and large, dark eyes.

Mr. Dobbs came hurrying up beside her. "I don't think this one will do, miss. He's a young stallion and a little spirited for an inexperienced young rider." Ginny drew back as the chestnut flattened his ears against his head and snapped at

Mr. Dobbs with his lips drawn back, teeth showing.

"Take your arm off, that one would," muttered Mr. Dobbs. "Don't know why I keep him. But I love them all, you know." He smiled at Ginny's mother. Ginny walked away angrily. If he loved his ponies all that much, why didn't he take better care of them?

There was one other possibility down at the far end of the barn. Ginny could just barely see it, but the pony at least looked tall enough for her. Mr. Dobbs dashed past her with a rope in his hand. "I'll show you a good one," he said. "This is the best in the barn. Very gentle," he said to Ginny's mother, who was still looking a little shaken by the performance of the bad-tempered chestnut. "And this one is just the right size for your little girl." He plunged into the stall and backed the pony out.

Ginny's heart sank. This was her last chance, the only other pony of suitable size left in this awful barn, and it was a miserable sight. The pony was so many colors that, through her haze of disappointment, Ginny couldn't make out what they all were until Mr. Dobbs had shoved a

bridle on the pony's head and led it outside.

It was a mare, Ginny discovered, and under the dirt and grime she was white with large patches of dark brown spots. Her tail was black, her mane was white, and the forelock that almost covered her eyes was as black as her tail. Ginny went up to the pony and offered her a lump of sugar from the pocket of her blue jeans. The pony accepted it and ate it slowly, turning her head to look at the little Shetlands in the field behind the fence.

"Why, she's blind in one eye!" gasped Ginny.

"No, miss, she's not blind. She's got one brown eye and one blue one, but just because they don't match doesn't mean she can't see perfectly well. Makes her look a bit special, don't you think? Come on, then, up you go!" Before Ginny knew what was happening, he had boosted her up onto the pony's thin bare back and put the reins into her hands. "Off you go and give her a try. Enjoy yourself."

Ginny glanced at her mother, who was smiling. "You look very nice on her, dear," she said. Ginny smiled back. But her face felt stiff, as though the smile would crack it. She turned her attention to the thin pony under her. "Come on, you poor

8

creature," she said under her breath to the waiting pony. "Let's get this over."

They slopped through the mud and found firmer ground over by the edge of the field. It had been ages since Ginny had last ridden—not since last September, which suddenly seemed a long time ago. She had never been allowed to ride without a saddle at camp, and the pony felt very different and bony and strange under her. She took a handful of the pony's white mane in one hand, and squeezed with her legs.

The pony started to trot. Much to Ginny's surprise she found that the trot was smooth and that she was having no trouble staying on. She pulled on the reins and the pony obediently came back to a walk. Then Ginny asked her to canter. The dead wet grass squelched under the pony's hoofs as she cantered slowly beside the wire fence. Ginny slid a little from side to side, but finally managed to balance in the middle. She pulled the pony back to a walk, turned her, and cantered back to where her mother and Mr. Dobbs were waiting by the barn door.

"Lovely, dear," said her mother.

"Nice little mare," said Mr. Dobbs.

The spotted pony stood still, with her head down, as worn out as she might have been by an hour's hard ride. It had finally started to snow, and Ginny could see the flakes melting in the pony's dirty mane. She could feel her own soggy braids dripping down her shoulders and soaking through her jacket.

There was a silence. Both her mother and Mr. Dobbs were looking at Ginny expectantly. In spite of all the dampness, Ginny's mouth felt dry. She discovered in one quick moment that disappointment seemed to have a funny taste.

"She is a nice pony, Mr. Dobbs," Ginny said at last. "She'll be just perfect." She slid off the pony's back without looking and landed in icy mud up to her ankles.

Mr. Dobbs beamed. "A little spring grass will have her fattened up in no time," he said cheerfully. "Hay gets poor at this time of year." Ginny turned away, afraid her dislike would show in her face. She knew there was no excuse for the ponies to look so thin and miserable, whatever the time of year.

Mr. Dobbs led the pony back into the barn.

Ginny stood and watched the pony go, noticing sadly how thin she was, how her sharp hipbones stuck out, and how her drooping black tail hung down full of mud and burrs.

"There you go, dream pony," she said to herself. "But at least I'll just have you for the summer. I'm not stuck with you forever. And you are a whole lot better than no pony at all."

Chaper Two

The morning sunlight splashed through the window onto Ginny's face. Only half awake, she buried her face in the pillow and pushed her feet down to a cooler spot between the sheets.

Morning. Wednesday. *Wednesday morning*. She sat up, suddenly wide awake. Today was the day the pony was to come.

Ginny looked across the room at the shelves jammed with stories about horses and ponies and books on how to ride and care for them. On the top shelf her collection of glass and china horses sparkled in the sunlight.

Ginny grinned as she swung out of bed. It was a good thing she'd dusted her miniature horses just a few days ago, because they would not get the attention this summer they had always been given before. The tiny horses would have to wait, frozen in their artificial prancing across the white shelf. Ugly and shabby as the summer pony was, at least she was real.

Everything was ready. Ginny's father, complaining about having to leave his car outside all summer, had, nevertheless, cheerfully built a temporary stall for the pony at the back of the garage, near a window. Ginny still shuddered at the memory of the dark, airless barn where they had found the pony on that dreary day in March.

But that had been a month ago. Now the grass was beginning to turn green and there were small, sprouting leaves on the trees. The days were getting longer, and summer was almost here.

Two clean new metal garbage cans, with tight-fitting lids to discourage field mice, stood in the garage, filled with oats and a mixture of grains which the feed dealer had called "sweet feed" and promised would "fatten up a fence rail."

There were six bales of hay and five bales of straw; one bale of straw had already been opened and spread into a deep, golden bed in the stall. There was a heavy black rubber feed tub hanging in one corner of the stall, and a bucket for water in another. A brick of salt in a holder had been fastened to the wall near the feed tub, and a box of brushes, with a mane comb and hoof pick, stood on a shelf near the window.

Everything was ready and waiting—but there was still school today. Ginny groaned. The pony wasn't to be delivered until late afternoon, well after school was over for the day, and there was really nothing more to do but wait.

Riding on the school bus, then sitting through her classes, Ginny found her thoughts swinging between excitement and despair. The pony was an awful-looking thing. But maybe, after her shabby winter coat had finished shedding out and she'd had some proper food and good care, she might look a little better.

Ginny wished she could talk to someone about

it, but none of her classmates had the least interest in anything to do with horses. Ginny drew a row of pony heads down the margin of her math paper. The spotted pony would never look like Pam Jennings's pony, of course. *Her* pony was beautiful, half Thoroughbred and half Welsh, and was the color of a new copper penny. It had won unbelievable numbers of ribbons and championships everywhere. . . .

Ginny shut her eyes and tried to squeeze the thought of this pony from her head. Pam was a stuck-up thing, anyway, she'd heard, so who cared? Though they were the same age, and lived quite near each other, the two girls went to different schools and had never met. But Ginny had seen Pam and her pony at a number of local shows. That was the kind of pony, she admitted to herself gloomily, that she had wanted for herself this summer.

Ginny stared down at the paper on her desk and realized dimly that she'd drawn the pony heads in the margin with ink. She'd never be able to erase them. With a bored sigh, she began to copy her math problems on a fresh sheet of paper. She chewed thoughtfully on the end of one braid and stared blankly out of the school-room window. She felt absolutely sure the morning would never end.

The school bus eventually brought her home. Four o'clock came, and then five. Mr. Dobbs was late. Ginny's mother was making remarks about having to start dinner, Daddy would be home soon, had Ginny set the table?—but Ginny barely heard and paid no attention. She felt as though her ears had grown stiff listening for the sound of truck wheels on the driveway.

Ginny and her mother heard it at the same moment—the clashing of gears, the rattling of a tired engine, and the sound of tires on the drive. They flew out the back door as a battered green pickup truck, with high board sides, stopped outside the garage.

"Evening there, Mrs. Anderson. Got your pony here, safe and sound." Mr. Dobbs went to the back of the truck, opened it, and disappeared inside. Ginny could barely breathe. She heard thumping sounds and Mr. Dobbs called out "Whoa!" in a loud voice. Suddenly the pony's head appeared at the back of the truck. Mr.

16

Dobbs shouted "Whoa!" again, but the pony paid no attention. With her eyes on the green grass growing close beside the driveway, she took one impatient sliding step and jumped out of the truck.

Thin and hungry as she was, weak and shaky from the ride in the unfamiliar truck, the pony stumbled as she landed. Her knees buckled, and she fell. Lying there on the grass, without even picking up her head, she began to eat.

Ginny and her mother stood, frozen with astonishment, staring at the exhausted, half-starved pony lying in a heap on their lawn. The embarrassed Mr. Dobbs rushed to the pony's head and tugged at her halter until, with a tired sigh, she got slowly to her feet.

"There we are!" cried Mr. Dobbs. He thrust the pony's frayed lead rope into Ginny's hand. Ginny just managed a stiff, polite smile. Mr. Dobbs took a folded check from Ginny's mother and buttoned it carefully in the pocket of his shirt.

He drove off quickly in his clattering truck. "He's afraid we might change our minds," Ginny thought bitterly. She and her mother looked in silence at the thin, shabby pony standing pa-

17

tiently in the driveway, with her brown ears pricked and her tattered black forelock cascading over her unmatching eyes.

"How nice to have a pony here at last," said Mrs. Anderson.

"Wonderful," said Ginny, hoping fiercely that she sounded more cheerful than she really felt inside. "Gosh, I forgot to ask Mr. Dobbs what her name is. Come on, old girl," and she led the tired pony into her new stall.

"Perhaps you could name her Patches?" suggested Mrs. Anderson that evening after dinner. Ginny leaned over the side of the stall, gazing at the pony thoughtfully, noticing that she'd finished all her hay and had started hungrily to eat her straw bed.

"Do you mean that moke belongs to *us*?" Ginny's father, who was being introduced to the pony for the first time, sounded as though he was trying not to laugh.

"She does not belong to us," Ginny said quickly. "She's only here for the summer. And what is a moke, anyway?" She wanted to distract her father's attention from the looks of the pony before he laughed out loud, and though she didn't really care what a moke was, she knew the best way to change any subject with a grownup was to ask a question.

Mr. Anderson started to fill his pipe. "When I was a boy I had a friend who came from England. He used to tell us about a donkey he had at home and he called it a moke. Great word. Moke. I always liked it." He studied the pony with amused interest. "Does it eat like that all the time, or does it stop sometimes to rest?"

Ginny was grateful for the soft light over the stall. The pony's ribs and hipbones didn't show up as clearly as they did in daylight. Though she had to agree the pony wasn't much to look at, it wasn't the pony's fault, and she didn't think she could bear it if anyone laughed at her now.

Ginny was tired and confused, yet it really was wonderful having a pony, even this one. She picked up a fresh armful of hay and piled it in the corner of the stall. "Here, you silly old moke," she said in a shaky voice. "This is better for you to eat than straw."

Ginny's father gave her a quick hug. "Go to bed. You're asleep on your feet. Your moke will still be here in the morning."

Chapter Three

It was barely daylight the next morning when Ginny slipped out of bed and tiptoed quietly downstairs in her bathrobe and slippers. She took a carrot from the refrigerator and went out to the garage.

The pony was really there. She turned her head

toward Ginny and nickered softly in a gentle sound of welcome. Ginny tried not to feel pleased. She knew the pony was just asking to be fed, but it felt nice to be greeted so warmly anyway. She gave the carrot to the pony and patted her on her shaggy neck.

Everything smelled so good. The whole garage smelled of fresh spring morning, of the new wood of the stall, and of hay, and feed, and pony— Ginny shut her eyes and drew in a long, deep breath. There was no question about it. This just had to be the most wonderful smell in the world.

The pony banged her hoof impatiently against the stall door. Ginny laughed and hurried to fill a small wooden measure with oats and sweet feed. She poured it into the feed tub in the stall and watched as the pony, with a sigh of pleasure, started to eat.

One quart of grain didn't look like much to Ginny, but the manager of the feed store had warned her to be careful. "If this pony of yours is as thin as you tell me," he had said, "you can be sure she hasn't seen a grain of oats in a long time. You take a pony in that condition and throw the good feed into her, you'll kill her for sure. What they call killing by kindness. Good hay won't hurt her, and all the fresh, clean water she'll drink, but take it easy with the grain."

The pony chased the last oat around the bottom of the feed tub, ate it, and waited impatiently while Ginny brought her an armload of hay.

It took forty-five minutes for Ginny to put the bridle on the pony later that morning. Ginny struggled with the tangle of straps and bit that had looked like a bridle when Mr. Dobbs had handed it to her the evening before; somehow it had become a confused handful of leather and buckles since she had lifted it down from its hook that morning.

Ginny had bridled one or two horses at camp before, but only with a counselor standing beside her, and the bridle given to her in proper order, reins just so, headpiece in one hand, bit hanging tidily where it belonged. Everything was different now that she was alone.

Annoyed and impatient with herself, Ginny finally sat on a bale of hay, put the bridle down, and straightened out the jumble of leather. Once she had it looking like a bridle again, she remembered how to slip the bit into the patient pony's mouth and the headpiece over her ears. Flushed with triumph, she buckled the throatlatch and led the pony out of the stall.

Her father and mother were waiting to see her off on her first ride. "Don't you have a saddle for the moke?" asked Mr. Anderson as Ginny wiggled up onto the pony's bare back.

"I didn't see one, so I guess not," said Ginny, "unless Mr. Dobbs gave it to Mother when I was holding the pony yesterday." But her mother shook her head. "I can't see what possible difference it could make anyway," said Ginny. "The pony's not about to buck me off or run away with me. She hasn't got that much energy, I shouldn't think."

"Ginny's probably right," said Mrs. Anderson. "We can always arrange to get one later on if she needs one, I suppose."

Mr. Anderson gave the pony a friendly slap on her shaggy rump. "On your way, then, and have a good ride, you two."

Ginny shortened her reins nervously and squeezed the pony with her legs. Much to her relief, the pony swung off at a willing walk, her

24

head up and her ears pricked cheerfully. Ginny didn't quite dare take one hand off the reins to wave, so she smiled stiffly over her shoulder at her parents instead, then turned and rode the pony down the drive.

The pony stopped obediently at the road to let a car go by, then walked on promptly when she was asked. Ginny began to relax, and was even able to laugh at herself when she saw how tightly her hands had been gripping the reins. In a short time they were in the woods, and the familiar paths Ginny had walked so often in the past opened suddenly into a fresh and wonderful world.

Everything looked completely new and different from the back of the pony. There was cheerful activity in the woods that Ginny had never noticed before. The squirrels and chipmunks went about their busy lives, undisturbed by the muffled sound of the pony's hoofs on the loamy paths. And then, to Ginny's incredulous delight, a doe, with her very young and still wobbling fawn beside her, stood in a sunny clearing and did not turn away when the pony caught sight of them and stopped. The doe and the pony looked at each other, unafraid. Ginny sat absolutely still, hardly daring to breathe, making no movement that might startle the deer. Finally the doe turned her lovely head to nuzzle her fawn, and led it soundlessly into the deeper shadows of the woods.

They came to the stream that crossed the path and Ginny let the pony stop in the middle to drink. The pony took a few swallows, then began pawing the water. Ginny clutched at the reins with alarm and then realized, with amusement, that the pony was just playing with the water, enjoying the splashing sound and the sprays of water flying from her pawing hoof.

Suddenly the pony's knees buckled and the next thing Ginny knew she was standing in the middle of the stream with the icy water halfway up to her knees, the reins still in one hand, and the pony lying, with obvious enjoyment, in the water beside her.

Ginny squished over to a rock beside the stream, put her head in her hands, and laughed until she cried. Finally she stood up, pushed her braids back over her shoulder, wiped her eyes, and gave the reins a determined tug. The pony blinked her eyes and scrambled to her feet, shak-

ing herself like a dog and spraying water in all directions.

"That was a ridiculous performance!" gasped Ginny, laughing and shivering as she tried to dodge out of the way of the drops of water. "Cut that out, you idiot pony! That water is *cold*." She flung herself onto the pony's wet back and urged her into a brisk trot, then into a canter. When they burst-out of the woods into the warmer sunlight of an open field, Ginny, still laughing, pulled the pony back to a walk and patted her on the neck.

It wasn't until several minutes later, as they walked and dried out in the sun, that Ginny suddenly realized that her nervousness was gone. She had forgotten to worry about her riding. She would get along very well—at least, she reminded herself with a grin, if she remembered to keep the pony moving when they crossed a stream.

Ginny and the pony drifted across the field, enjoying the warmth of the spring sun. The whole golden summer stretched ahead. A little bit stiff and sore, relaxed and happy, Ginny turned her pony's head toward home.

Chapter Four

It took three separate soapy baths in a row, and numberless heavy buckets of warm water, to get the pony clean. On the first warm Saturday morning, Ginny carried the buckets down the kitchen steps to where the pony was tied under the blossoming branches of a small

29

apple tree. She rubbed the suds into the pony's coat and mane and tail, rinsed her off, and washed her again. Ginny was soaking wet herself; her shirt and blue jeans and sneakers were splashed with suds and water, but she didn't mind. The pony looked much better as she stood dripping in the sun. A lot of her shaggy winter coat had come out with the scrubbing. Her white markings were now spotless, and the brown patches were beginning to shine a warm, chocolate color as she dried.

Ginny sat down to catch her breath on the bottom kitchen step. But she jumped to her feet a moment later, startled to hear someone calling her name. "Ginny? Hi! My name is Pam Jennings. Our place isn't very far from here; did you know we're practically neighbors? May I see your new pony?"

And it really was Pam Jennings coming around the corner of the house, holding an apple in her hand.

Ginny would have recognized Pam anywhere from watching her ride her beautiful pony at so many shows. "Hi. Oh, gosh, I'm a mess. I'm Ginny Anderson. How nice of you to come." Ginny

stumbled over the words. "The pony's not really mine. I just have her for the summer. She's kind of a mess, too, right now. I've just given her a bath."

"She looks lovely." The dark-haired girl offered the apple to the pony, who bit into it gently. "She has nice manners. Are you planning to show her this summer?"

Ginny just shook her head wordlessly, wild pictures racing through her mind of rows of elegant show ponies in a ring and everyone laughing at her thin, shabby, strangely marked pony beside them.

"That's too bad." Pam stroked the pony's wet head. "It would be fun to have someone to go with. But at least we can ride together, can't we? There's no one nearby who has a pony. I was so glad when the feed man told Michael there was finally another pony in the neighborhood." She rubbed the pony's wet ears. "Michael takes care of Firefly, my pony, and my mother's and father's horses." Ginny had no idea what to say, so she just nodded.

"What do you call her?" asked Pam.

"Her name is Mokey." There. It was said, out

loud. Like so many nicknames, this one had stuck. For days everyone in the family had called the pony "the moke," and then, one day, she was Mokey.

Pam gave the wet pony a final pat on the shoulder. "Good-by, Mokey. I have to go now. Mother is waiting in the car. Do you want to meet tomorrow morning at my place for a ride, Ginny? About eleven o'clock?"

"Okay," Ginny said faintly as Pam hurried away. Ginny collapsed again onto the bottom of the kitchen steps and stared, chin in her hands, at her spotted pony half asleep under the tree. "It will be great fun," she said to herself firmly. "But—oh, dear. Mokey, I wish you were just a little bit more elegant." She made a face at the idea of Mokey plodding along behind the light-footed Firefly, Pam riding so beautifully in her well-cut jodhpurs and shining brown boots, while she rode bareback in blue jeans and sneakers.

At the same time, Ginny knew she was being unfair. Pam really had seemed very nice, and though Ginny loved riding alone with Mokey, it would be pleasant to have company once in a while to share some of the fun. She got up, unclipped the rope from Mokey's halter, and turned her loose to graze on the lawn.

"But don't you lie down and roll and get yourself dirty," she told the pony fiercely. "You may not be beautiful, but at least you can be clean."

Mokey did roll, of course, luxuriating in the feeling of the sun-warmed grass on her drying coat. When she got up and shook herself triumphantly, she had grass stains all over the white parts of her coat, and some in her mane, and she needed another bath. The back yard looked like a battlefield when they were finished; the lawn under the apple tree was a small sea of soapsuds and great chunks of earth had been scooped up out of the lawn where the pony had rolled, digging her hoofs into the ground.

Ginny walked Mokey dry, tied her up in her stall, and surveyed the damaged lawn gloomily. Somehow, she felt, this was going to be one of those days she would be glad to see end.

Her father was furious, of course, at the holes in the lawn and her mother was annoyed at the splashes of soapy water on the kitchen floor. As soon as she could, Ginny bridled her pony and set off down the driveway at a brisk trot. Mokey swung along cheerfully with her head up and her ears pricked, as glad as Ginny to be out for a ride.

When they got home and Ginny slid off Mokey's back, her father was waiting, smoking his pipe and looking, Ginny was glad to notice, much more cheerful than he had when she had last seen him, rolling the lumps out of the lawn.

Ginny brushed the mud and dust off Mokey's legs. Her father was holding the pony's reins and, Ginny noticed with surprise, was patting Mokey's neck.

"I thought you said you didn't like horses," said Ginny with a smile.

Mokey nudged Mr. Anderson's arm with her soft muzzle and he began to rub her behind the ears in her favorite spot. "I don't like horses and ponies in general, but I think I like this one in particular," said Mr. Anderson. "And I'm glad you're having such a good time with her. But, Ginny, you must keep her off the lawn! You know that big oak tree down the hill beyond the house, just where the lawn ends? Why can't you tie her to that tree with a rope and let her eat the long grass down there?"

35

"I think that sounds like a wonderful idea," said Ginny. Her father got a rope from the garage and the two of them led the pony down the hill, tied one end of the rope to her halter and the other around the trunk of the tree. The grass was lush and tall and Mokey started grazing contentedly.

Ginny and her father walked back up toward the house and turned for a moment to enjoy the sight of the pony, relaxed and happy, grazing quietly under the tree.

Suddenly, as they were watching, Mokey seemed to go mad. She flung herself into the air on her hind legs, crashed to the ground, staggered to her feet, and fell again. Ginny started to run toward her as fast as she could.

She didn't hear her father shouting or his footsteps running to catch up with her. As she reached the thrashing pony, her father's strong hand on her shoulder threw her backward so that she tripped and fell. "Let me go!" she screamed at her father. "Something awful's the matter with Mokey!"

"Stay away from that pony!" her father shouted. "Stop it, Ginny! You can't go near her now! She's in such a panic she'll kick you to pieces!" Ginny struggled to her feet and stood still for a moment, gasping for breath. They could see now what had happened. As the pony had moved at the end of the long rope, it had twisted around her hind legs, frightening her into a panic. She had fought the rope wildly until she had been thrown down on the ground, foaming with sweat from fear and exhaustion.

Now the pony was lying still. Only her sides were heaving as she gasped for air. "Move quietly," Ginny's father said in a low voice. "I don't know much about horses, but panic is pretty much the same in any living thing. Go to her head, Ginny. Stay out of the way of her hoofs. Talk to her and see if you can keep her quiet. I'll get a knife to cut the rope."

Ginny knelt in the grass by the pony's head, her common sense slowly coming back. Knowing her father was right, she was ready to jump to her feet, out of the way, if the terrified pony should start to fight again.

But Mokey seemed almost unconscious. Her eyes were glazed and her breath rasped in her throat. She did not try to move even when

Ginny's father came back and started to cut the tangled rope with a sharp knife.

The rope finally lay in pieces on the ground. "Why doesn't she get up?" said Ginny, her voice shaking. "She's free now, but she doesn't seem to know it!"

Mr. Anderson pulled a last piece of rope away from the pony's front leg. "I wonder if she's in some kind of shock," he said. "Ginny, talk to her. Try to make her get up."

"Maybe her legs are broken," sobbed Ginny, the tears she had been fighting pouring down her cheeks at last. "I've never seen anything so awful in my life! Get up, Mokey, get *up*!"

But the pony just lay flat on her side, her legs limp and her head stretched out on the ground. Ginny became dimly aware that her mother was standing beside her. "I saw it from the house," she said. "John, do you think the pony could have broken her back?"

"If she hasn't, we're lucky," Mr. Anderson said grimly. "Come on, old girl, try to get up." He gave the pony's halter a gentle pull.

Mokey moved. She blinked her eyes and lifted her head. Slowly, with enormous effort, she put out one foreleg, then another. "That's it! Good!"

said Mr. Anderson. "Stand away from her now. Give her room."

The pony rested for a few minutes, turning her head weakly as though finding her way back from a dream. Ginny could see blood on the pony's legs, just above her hoofs and behind her knees. She took a deep breath but kept still.

Then, suddenly, the pony surged to her feet, staggering a little but bearing weight on all four legs. She took one step forward, and then another. The pony lowered her head, shook herself like a dog, and started peacefully to graze.

Ginny burst into tears again. "I never saw anything so stupid!" she said. "Five minutes ago we thought she was dead, and now she's eating as though nothing happened at all!"

Mr. Anderson shook his head. "Amazing," he said. "I'm beginning to think that caring for a pony is not quite as simple as one might imagine."

"Bring her along up to the house, Ginny," said Mrs. Anderson. "She's got some pretty bad rope burns on her legs. We'll have to take care of them. I have some healing ointment that should be just right."

Ginny sighed. Her knees were still shaking

from her fear and the relief of knowing her pony was going to be all right. "We've got an awful lot to learn, Mokey," she said. "I hope you can live through it."

Slowly, for Mokey was very stiff and sore, they made their way back up the hill.

Chapter Five

Mokey's legs were painfully swollen the next day, but both Ginny and her mother, after inspecting the rope burns anxiously in the brighter light of morning, agreed that they did not look any worse than they had the night before.

They put more ointment on every sore place they could find, then Ginny led the pony slowly down to the long grass near the oak tree and let her graze in the sun.

It was almost eleven o'clock when Ginny glanced at her watch and remembered with horror that she was supposed to meet Pam for a ride. Mokey would not be hurried back up the hill to the stall in the garage; it hurt her too much to walk fast, and she did not want to be shut up, anyway. Ginny finally coaxed her into her stall and rushed to the telephone.

Pam had left the house by then, of course. Ginny groaned under her breath. "It is terribly important that Pam gets this message," Ginny said urgently. "I was supposed to ride with her today, but—" She stopped, too embarrassed to admit what had happened. "Could you just tell her, please, that my pony is a little lame this morning, and that I will call her again some time soon."

The courteous voice on the other end of the phone said that the message would be sent to the stables immediately. Ginny hung up, feeling both guilty and relieved. Maybe by the time she saw Pam again Mokey would be completely well and no one outside the family would ever have to know how dumb she had been to let her own pony get hurt.

It was several days before Mokey could walk easily again. "The only reason she's not actually lame," Ginny told her mother gloomily, "is that all her legs hurt so much that she doesn't know where to limp the most." Ginny led her pony at a slow walk for a half hour twice a day; gradually the swelling disappeared and the burns began to heal.

Ginny caught a glimpse of Pam in town one morning. They both smiled politely at each other and said "hello," but neither girl said anything more. Ginny's mother gave her daughter a quick look. "Wasn't that the Jennings girl?" she asked. "I didn't know you knew her."

"I don't. Not really, I mean," said Ginny awkwardly. She didn't try to explain about the ride that had been forgotten in the worry over Mokey. It all sounded too idiotic, she thought to herself angrily. The whole situation had been idiotic, and she simply did not want to talk about it.

Mokey was much better, anyway; that was all

43

that really mattered. The last of her shabby winter coat had finally shed out, leaving her smooth and shining, though to Ginny's anxious eye she still looked thin. Her black tail, now free of mats and burrs, grew long and full, and her white mane and black forelock at last gave up their tangles to Ginny's careful brushing.

The day after the accident with the rope, Ginny's father ordered what looked to Ginny like a mountain of posts and rails and dug endless deep holes with grim determination until a wide-fenced paddock surrounded the big oak. When the last rail had been slid into place, Ginny led Mokey through the gate and turned her loose with a flourish.

"My back is never going to be the same again," said Mr. Anderson cheerfully. "But it looks very nice, and Mokey will be safe. She's looking great, Ginny. You're doing a wonderful job with her."

The whole family leaned on the top rail and watched proudly as the pony, delighted with her freedom, cantered across the paddock, stopped to lie down and roll, and then began to graze.

It was hot that afternoon. Instead of walking

Mokey up and down the driveway as she had been doing, Ginny decided to lead her along the path through the woods where it was much cooler. Their feet made hardly any sound on the deep loamy path and it was a sudden surprise when a tall chestnut pony with his rider whirled around a bend in the path and came to a violent stop in front of them.

The chestnut pony half-reared and tried to spin around. The girl on his back dropped her hands and held him steady without seeming to move in the saddle. "Stop it, you nitwit pony," his rider said calmly. "Ginny, hi! What happened? Did you have a fall?"

Ginny shook her head. "Gosh, I'm sorry we surprised your pony like this," she finally managed to say. "I'm fine. It's good to see you again."

Pam dismounted, patted her dancing pony soothingly on his sweaty neck, and led him toward Ginny and Mokey. "If you and Mokey are both fine, how come you aren't riding?" There was no mistaking the genuine concern in Pam's voice, and suddenly Ginny was telling her the whole story.

"So, you see," she finished awkwardly, "I felt

like an awful fool about the whole thing. And I'm not sure whether I should ride Mokey or not. Those darned burns still look pretty ghastly."

"You know what you could do if you'd like," said Pam. "You could bring her over to our place and ask Michael. He's been with horses so long he'd know what to do."

"It would be wonderful, if you don't think he'd mind," said Ginny gratefully. Leading their ponies, the two girls went through a white gate, across a wide field, and into the stable yard.

Red geraniums bloomed in white wooden tubs on the low wall around the yard; lovely shining heads of several horses looked over the low doors with serene interest in the new arrivals. At the sound of hoofs on the smoothly raked gravel yard, a man of medium height, with a touch of gray in his hair and the keenest blue eyes Ginny had ever seen, came out through the open doors in the center of stable.

"Hi, Michael, it's okay. I didn't fall off," said Pam quickly. "I found a friend in the woods. She needs some advice. Ginny, this is Michael."

"Hello." Ginny and Michael smiled at each other, then Michael turned to take the chestnut

47

pony's reins. "He's hot, Miss Pam," Michael said reprovingly. "I'll sponge him off and cool him out first."

"He fusses all the time when he's by himself," said Pam. "He's not much fun to ride alone."

The chestnut pony danced his way across the stable yard with Michael walking quietly at his head. Ginny noticed that he limped slightly.

"Michael was a steeplechase jockey in England for years," Pam explained to Ginny as they sat on the low wall to wait. "He had a terrible fall so he can't be a jockey anymore, but he can still ride terrifically, and he's great with horses." The two girls sat swinging their legs comfortably on the warm stones; Mokey nibbled without much interest on a geranium leaf, then stood quietly, the ends of the reins in Ginny's hand.

It did not seem long before Michael came back. "Now, then," he said briskly. "What seems to be the problem?"

Though he asked polite questions and left time for Ginny's answers, Ginny could tell that he had seen everything in his first sweeping look at her pony. He bent over and picked up Mokey's front leg, let the hoof down gently, patted the pony, and said to Ginny, "Bring her along inside. We'll soon fix her up."

It was cool and quiet in the wide aisle between the two rows of stalls. Mokey stood patiently, looking around her with interest. The brass rings beside the stalls were glowing softly with polish; a darkly shining leather halter with a brass nameplate hung beside each stall door. Behind the dark wood paneling and black iron grille that enclosed each enormous stall, Ginny could just see the heads of the gleaming horses and could hear them moving about quietly in their deep, clean beds of straw.

Michael came up to Mokey with a small clipping machine hardly bigger than his hand. He let Mokey sniff at it, then plugged it in and switched it on. It made almost no sound. Mokey blew at it suspiciously once or twice, then relaxed and paid no attention as Michael, talking quietly to the pony, began to move it gently near her muzzle.

"We'll just let her get used to it for a bit," he said. "I doubt this pony has ever seen a clipping machine before. Have you had her long, Miss Ginny?"

Ginny told him about Mokey and watched, fascinated, as Michael clipped the long hairs from Mokey's muzzle, trimmed the insides and edges of her ears, and started to clip away at her mane, just behind her ears.

"You're not going to cut it all off!" gasped Ginny.

"No, silly," laughed Pam. "Only that little bit where the bridle goes behind her ears. It keeps the mane much tidier. Michael does it to all our horses."

Michael patted Mokey approvingly. "Nice little mare," he said. "Has a lot of sense. Now, let's get to these fetlocks of yours." He ran the clipping machine over the round joints above Mokey's hoofs and the shaggy hair fell away. He clipped around the burns below the fetlocks, went to get a bucket of warm water, and gently sponged the sore places. When the hair had dried, he clipped above the hoofs again, and finally, nodding with satisfaction, straightened up and switched off the clipping machine.

"Getting all that hair away from those burns will help them heal more quickly," he said to Ginny. "I'll give you a jar of a different kind of

ointment. Use it lightly, just a very little bit, once a day." He put the clippers away and went to get the ointment.

When he came back, he gave Ginny a jar and a small white plastic container. "Give her this powder in her feed tonight," he said. "I shouldn't imagine this pony's been wormed for some time. This medicine should help her pick up and look better very soon."

"She looks so much nicer already after what you've done," said Ginny. "Thank you so much. I had no idea how much difference clipping those little bits could make."

"Now, don't rush off just yet," said Michael. "Two more things. You can ride her now. Just go easy for another day or two. And this pony needs shoeing. Badly. Do you see how long her toes have grown, and how they are chipping around the edges?"

"Gosh," said Ginny, kneeling to inspect the chips that Michael pointed out to her. "I hadn't thought about that. Mr. Dobbs didn't even mention it. Do you suppose she's ever had shoes on in her life? Why don't those chipped places turn into cracks?"

"They will if she isn't shod," said Michael. "The blacksmith is coming here tomorrow morning to reset a shoe on Mr. Jennings's black colt. Would you like to bring your pony over and let him see to her if he has the time?"

Ginny felt her face getting red. "I feel I'm being an awful pest," she said finally. "You've been so nice and taken so much time this afternoon. I don't want to get in your way."

"Don't be ridiculous," Pam said quickly. "Michael never minds when someone really wants to learn about horses, do you, Michael?"

"But there seems to be so much I don't know," said Ginny, looking at her pony despairingly.

"You will never feel you know enough," Michael agreed cheerfully. "No matter how many years you spend with horses, there will always be something new to learn. That's what makes them so interesting. Off you go now, you two, I've other work to get done. You will have your pony here for the blacksmith in the morning, Miss Ginny?"

Ginny smiled gratefully. "We'll be here," she promised.

Chapter Six

Mokey did not like the pink powdered medicine in her grain that evening. She rattled the feed tub with her muzzle, then blew through her nostrils in annoyance at the strange taste and tried to eat the oats without getting any of the powder. But by the time Ginny went to say good night to her before going to bed, all the grain and the medicine had been eaten.

Neither did Mokey like the sight of the smoke from the blacksmith's fire the next morning. She slid to a stop and threw her head in the air when she trotted around the corner of the stable and saw the blacksmith's truck with the hot coals in a portable metal stand beside it. Ginny nearly went off over Mokey's shoulder but managed to save herself by clutching wildly at the shaggy mane.

The blacksmith made disapproving noises when he examined Mokey's hoofs. The pony, after a few suspicious snorts, stood quietly while the blacksmith trimmed each hoof with a thin-bladed curved knife and a heavy file.

"Been some time since this pony's been seen to," the blacksmith said finally, straightening up and frowning at Ginny. "Plain light shoe on this one, wouldn't you say, Michael?"

Michael, who had been putting the black colt back in his stall, came over, nodded good morning to Ginny, and went into murmured consultation with the blacksmith.

Ginny, who had not said a word during all this time, rubbed Mokey's ears, trying to hear what

the two men were saying, uncomfortably aware
that her shirttails had pulled out of the waist of
her blue jeans when she had nearly fallen off, and
thinking how funny her spotted pony with her
unmatched eyes and mane and tail must look
outside this perfectly kept stable full of blooded
and beautiful horses. She began to feel more and
more ridiculous as she stood beside her pony
while the two highly skilled and knowledgeable

men discussed each hoof with serious concentration.

"She's only a perfectly ordinary pony," Ginny wanted to say. "She isn't a show pony and she isn't a race horse, she's just Mokey." But she didn't say it, just watched in silence as the blacksmith picked up one hoof, held a shoe on it, shook his head, and went back to his truck for another.

"Toes in a little on the right foreleg," commented the blacksmith. "Soon mend that."

Almost two hours later, he set the last nail in the last shoe, stepped back from the pony, and waved his hand. "Jog her out," he commanded.

Ginny looked helplessly at Michael. "I don't know what that means," she whispered. Michael smiled and took Mokey's reins. "He wants to see her led at a trot to make sure she is moving evenly and straight," he said. "I'll take the pony." He clucked to Mokey, who had fallen half asleep, turned her, and led her away at a trot.

"I don't believe it," Ginny said out loud. "I simply don't believe it." For the first time that morning, the blacksmith grinned at her.

"Proper shoeing makes a bit of difference," he said briefly.

Ginny just stared. Mokey began to trot out

with a stride that seemed to lengthen with each step. Michael brought her back to a walk, turned her, and let her go into a trot again. Mokey arched her neck, gave a delighted swish of her tail, and seemed to float over the ground.

"Pony's not a bad mover," said the blacksmith. "Given a chance, that is. Don't forget, young lady, a pony's hoofs grow all the time, just like your fingernails. Only the poor pony has to stand on those hoofs, and they can get pretty sore when they aren't tended to. They grow uneven, and they chip and crack and change the whole angle of the leg when she moves. Now she's comfortable and the angle of the hoof is right, and it doesn't hurt any more when she strides out. Give her a few more months of proper shoeing and you'll see even more of a difference. Mind, this has to be done every five or six weeks."

Ginny gave the blacksmith her name and address for his billing records and thanked him and Michael gratefully. Mokey's hoofbeats made a new and musical sound as she jogged across the road on their way home.

Two weeks later, when Mokey's legs were completely healed, Ginny called Pam to suggest they ride together the next morning. Pam was regretful. "I'm sorry, but I can't tomorrow," she said. "Our new outside course is ready. They just finished putting in the stone wall yesterday, and Michael says that if I don't school Firefly over some new fences pretty soon, he's going to forget how to jump." Pam laughed. "Of course that's not true, but it has been a long time, and I'm going to school him tomorrow."

"Can I come and watch?" asked Ginny eagerly.

"Why, of course! See you tomorrow."

When Ginny rode Mokey to the schooling field the next morning, Pam was warming up her pony. She waved briefly and went back to concentrating on her work. Ginny slid off Mokey's back and let the pony graze at the end of the reins while she watched Firefly and his intent rider.

Michael arrived and Pam stopped her pony. Ginny leaned against Mokey's shoulder and listened while Michael gave instructions and Pam nodded, her expression serious and thoughtful. "Easy on, this first time over a new course," Michael finished.

Pam made a wide circle, broke the pony smoothly into a canter, then into a slightly faster but controlled hand gallop. Firefly pricked his ears, settling into an even, cadenced stride, and glided over the first jump. A rail fence, a white gate, a stone wall with a heavy log on its top— every jump was met with a prick of ears and businesslike attention, with Pam seeming barely to move in the saddle. When she finished the course and drew smoothly to a walk, her face was flushed with pleasure.

"Very nice," said Michael. "Not perfect, mind. You must make a wider turn after the post-and-rail fence, to give your pony a better chance to get straight at the gate. You like to cut your corners, Miss Pam. Take your time. *Think* your turns before you make them."

Pam practiced the turn between the two jumps three more times, walked her pony to rest him, then jumped twice more before Michael finally nodded his approval.

"Fine," he said. "A good beginning. We'll try again on Thursday."

Pam took off her hard black hunt cap and waved it in front of her hot face. "Why don't you take Mokey around once, Ginny?" she said. "It's a lovely course."

"Oh, gosh, no," said Ginny quickly. "Mokey is

fun to ride, but she's not much of a jumper. She gets up right close to a jump before she'll even try to take off, then kind of hops over it. I've tried her at home in the paddock and over fallen logs in the woods. I don't think she likes jumping at all."

"You'd better keep that pony walking, Miss Pam," said Michael. "He's hot. And as for your pony, Miss Ginny, I think your problem is that bit you've got on her."

"Oh." Ginny looked at the metal bit in Mokey's mouth. "I never paid much attention to it. This is the bridle that came with her, so I thought it was okay."

"This is a curb bit," said Michael, "It's a very severe bit, and I believe Mokey is afraid of it. When a pony jumps, it must stretch out its head and neck in the air, just as it takes off and during the flight over the fence. If the rider doesn't give the pony enough rein, or if the pony is afraid of the bit, it will put in a short stride in front of the fence and jump the way you described. It might be interesting to try her in a snaffle."

"What a wonderful idea," said Pam, who was listening as she walked her pony in a circle around them. "Do we still have that pony snaffle that we used on Firefly when he was younger?"

"I'm sure we do," said Michael. "I'll just have a look."

In a few minutes he was back with a bridle in his hand. Ginny, filled with excitement, had taken Mokey's old bridle off and the pony had wandered into the center of the field.

"You shouldn't have done that," said Pam with concern. "She'll run away!"

"Oh, no," said Ginny. "She'll come when I call her. She always does." She raised her voice, calling to her pony; Mokey swung away from the grass she was eating and came trotting over to Ginny.

"Fantastic," muttered Pam. She gave her sweating pony a light slap on the neck. "Did you see that, you nitwit? Next time you toss me off _____ _____ _____ _____ ing off the way get her used to it, then jump her over the low part of the rail fence. . . . Wait. Just a moment. Do you have a hunt cap?"

Ginny shook her head. Pam rode over and gave her cap to Ginny. "This should fit well enough," she said. Ginny pushed the hard, velvet-covered cap down on her head.

"It feels funny," she said.

"You'll get used to it very quickly," said Pam.

"You must *never* jump without a hard hat," said Michael firmly. "It will protect your head in case you have a fall. All set? Then give it a try."

Ginny flung herself on Mokey's back and urged her into a trot. The pony mouthed the light snaffle bit, tossed her head, and swung into a strong canter.

"Good!" called Michael. "Let her move on, Miss Ginny!" Ginny turned the pony toward the low fence.

stride and that, when she does, you will be with her. Once she's learned she can trust herself and trust you not to hurt her mouth, she'll surprise you with what she can do."

"Okay," said Ginny doubtfully. She grabbed hold of the mane, gave her pony a half-hearted kick, and they crept over the rail fence for the second time.

"No," said Michael. "Try again."

Everything then became a blur to Ginny. The hot, sunny field, the feeling of the reluctant pony under her, the hateful rail fence, and Michael's stern insistent voice. "No. No, *no*. That isn't good enough. Try it again."

Finally, on the verge of tears and in desperation, Ginny reached back and gave Mokey a stinging slap with her hand. Completely astonished, the pony galloped toward the fence, pricked her ears, and swept over it with a foot to spare.

"Wow!" said Ginny. "So that's what you meant!"

"Fantastic!" cried Pam.

"Again," said Michael, but this time he sounded pleased.

It was a wonderful morning. Ginny and Mokey

jumped fence after fence with growing confidence. Michael called out crisp instructions, Pam shrieked with delight at each jump, and when Ginny finally pulled up, speechless with pleasure, Michael was nodding with quiet satisfaction.

"You're on your way now," said Michael to Ginny. "But no more jumping until you've gotten yourself a hard hunt cap of your own. There are three rules of jumping which you must always keep in mind. Give your horse a chance, never jump without a hard hat, and never jump alone." He gave Mokey an approving pat. "You two girls get off those ponies now," he said. "They've done enough for one day."

Pam assured Ginny that the snaffle bridle could be Mokey's for the rest of the summer. The old pony bridle was cleaned and then banished to a dim corner of the garage.

In the days that followed the two girls rode together through the countryside, finding low walls and fences and fallen logs to jump. Some days Pam was busy with other plans, and Ginny rode alone, content in the companionship of her pony and the soft welcome stillness of the woods and open fields.

around them. "Do we still have that pony snaffle that we used on Firefly when he was younger?"

"I'm sure we do," said Michael. "I'll just have a look."

In a few minutes he was back with a bridle in his hand. Ginny, filled with excitement, had taken Mokey's old bridle off and the pony had wandered into the center of the field.

"You shouldn't have done that," said Pam with concern. "She'll run away!"

"Oh, no," said Ginny. "She'll come when I call her. She always does." She raised her voice, calling to her pony; Mokey swung away from the grass she was eating and came trotting over to Ginny.

"Fantastic," muttered Pam. She gave her sweating pony a light slap on the neck. "Did you see that, you nitwit? Next time you toss me off remember this, and don't go running off the way you do."

Firefly walked on, unconcerned, while Michael fitted the bridle carefully to Mokey's head, making sure the bit rested comfortably in her mouth. "This snaffle has a gentle action," he explained to Ginny. "Work her around a few minutes to get her used to it, then jump her over the low part of the rail fence. . . . Wait. Just a moment. Do you have a hunt cap?"

Ginny shook her head. Pam rode over and gave her cap to Ginny. "This should fit well enough," she said. Ginny pushed the hard, velvet-covered cap down on her head.

"It feels funny," she said.

"You'll get used to it very quickly," said Pam.

"You must *never* jump without a hard hat," said Michael firmly. "It will protect your head in case you have a fall. All set? Then give it a try."

Ginny flung herself on Mokey's back and urged her into a trot. The pony mouthed the light snaffle bit, tossed her head, and swung into a strong canter.

"Good!" called Michael. "Let her move on, Miss Ginny!" Ginny turned the pony toward the low fence.

Mokey shortened her stride, slowed as she reached the fence, and bounced over it awkwardly.

"Did you see that?" Ginny said despairingly. "She's hopeless."

"Nonsense," said Michael. "You must make her understand that she is to gallop and jump right in

"Go on with Mokey!" cried Pam, and Ginny, with sudden determination, gave the pony a touch of her heel. She could feel Mokey galloping, but time stood still. The bars of the green gate stood dark and clean against the cloudy sky, and then it was behind them and they were galloping across the next field with Mokey bucking with delight and Ginny, laughing and gasping for breath, hanging onto the mane.

Dizzy with triumph, Ginny finally pulled up and turned in time to see Firefly land over the gate and come cantering over to Mokey. "That was a big one," announced Pam with satisfaction.

It had started to rain. "I wonder," said Ginny as they rode quietly across the field and into the dripping woods, "if I will ever again, in my whole life, jump anything that looks as big as that great green gate did this morning." She rested one hand on Mokey's warm, wet shoulder. "That was only a cow back there in that field, you know. It wasn't a bull and I think we knew it all the time."

"Of course," agreed Pam.

Proud and contented, the girls and their ponies made their way home.

Chapter Seven

It was going to be another scorcher of a day. Ginny woke up and scowled at the sun which was rising in a great orange ball, proclaiming still another day of the heat wave. She slid out of bed and tugged on her clothes, stuffed her feet into a pair of sneakers and ran a brush through her long hair. If she was going to ride at all today, it was obvious that she'd better ride early, while the morning air was still cool.

She fastened her hair back with a rubber band, stuffed a few lumps of sugar into her blue jeans pocket as she tiptoed through the kitchen, took the bridle from the hook in the garage, and started down the hill to Mokey's paddock.

It had been so hot during these last few days, and the horse flies had gotten so bad, that Mokey had been spending the days in the coolness of her stall in the garage, and the nights out in the paddock. She had eaten every blade of grass in the paddock, right down to the bare earth, but Ginny gave her an armful of hay and a tub of fresh water every evening, and the pony seemed to enjoy the new arrangement.

"Mokey!" Ginny called softly. But there was no answering whinny. Ginny stopped at the paddock gate and called again. It took her several baffled moments to realize that there was no pony anywhere in the paddock; Mokey was gone.

Once she was over her first astonishment, Ginny saw the rails down in one panel of the fence and the faint trace of a track through the dew-soaked orchard grass outside the paddock, leading up toward the driveway.

After the first moment of alarm, Ginny smiled to herself. The pony had probably gone over to Pam's stable, looking for company. She went to get her bicycle out of the garage and found, to her annoyance, that the front tire was almost flat. It hadn't been used since the day Mokey came. She found the bicycle pump, fixed the tire, and set off down the driveway, finding it a strange feeling to be riding a bike again after so long and deciding, for the millionth time, that it was no substitute for a pony.

Humming softly under her breath, she rode along the road, watching for signs of hoofprints and looking on both sides for her wandering pony. But there were no signs of Mokey anywhere.

The Jennings horses were being fed. Ginny could hear the rumble of the feed cart in the aisle of the stable as she propped her bike against the wall and poked her head through the door. Michael was away on his vacation, and a strange young man was caring for the horses while he was away. "Morning," said Ginny. "I've lost my pony and I thought she might have come here."

"Sorry, miss, I haven't seen her." The young man came to the door and looked out over the surrounding fields. "But if she does show up, I'll be glad to put her in the extra stall and give you a call."

"That would be wonderful. Thanks." Ginny gave him her name and phone number, which he wrote down carefully on the note pad by the stable telephone.

Ginny sat on her bike for a few minutes, trying to make up her mind what to do next. Pam was away; her parents had come home and insisted she go with them for a few days in the mountains, so she couldn't help.

Ginny was beginning to worry, just a little. She had been so sure Mokey would have come to the Jennings stable to visit Firefly, and it was a surprising disappointment not to have found her here.

Ginny decided to ride home on the bridle path through the woods, in case Mokey had chosen that way to come. Roots and stones in the path that she had never noticed riding Mokey made bike-riding difficult, and she was cross and breathless when she came out on the road again without having seen so much as a hoofprint anywhere, even in the soft ground near the stream.

She rode home, flung the bike into the garage, and stormed into the kitchen, where her mother and father were having breakfast.

"That dumb pony has run away," she announced. "Vanished. In fact, she must have flown. I can't even find a hoofprint." Suddenly, to her horror, she felt tears stinging her eyes. "I don't even know where to look for her!"

"Breakfast," Mrs. Anderson said firmly. "At least a glass of milk. You can't go looking for ponies on an empty stomach. And then I think we should call the police."

"The *police*?" said Ginny, startled out of the threatening tears. "Whatever for?"

"Maybe someone has seen her," said Mr. Anderson. "If you found a strange pony wandering about in your vegetable garden, which is very likely where she will be found, wouldn't you notify the police? And does that pony *ever* stop eating?"

Ginny had to laugh. "That's probably why she got out," she admitted. "I think she pushed the fence rails down to get at the grass outside the paddock. There isn't any left at all inside the fence."

Though the police were courteous and interested, they had no word of a found pony. They promised to watch for her and to report any news as soon as it was received.

The hot day grew hotter and dragged on endlessly. Mr. Anderson pulled on his hiking boots and set out through the woods to look for Mokey. Mrs. Anderson drove around the neighboring roads in the car, leaving Ginny to answer the phone if anyone called. But there were no calls, and when Mrs. Anderson finally returned, shaking her head, Ginny went off on her bike again.

It was late afternoon. Ginny was so tired and worried that she felt almost numb, but anything was better than just sitting still, waiting for the telephone to ring.

She rode up a number of strange driveways and knocked on many doors. Everyone was kind and concerned, but no one had seen a lost brown-and-white spotted pony—or any other pony—that day.

There was a long, sweeping blue gravel driveway that led to a house that could barely be seen from the road. Ginny turned her bike through the stone pillars at the entrance and found her tired legs would not pedal her bike through the

73

deep gravel. She hesitated, then left her bike and walked toward the house on foot.

She came around a last sweep of the drive and stopped so quickly that she slid. Beside the house an attractive young woman was leaning on a low white fence which surrounded an apple orchard. And there, under the apple trees, eating as usual with complete unconcern, was Mokey.

The woman turned and smiled at Ginny. "Hello," she said in a warm, friendly voice. "Is this your pony? We've so enjoyed having her with us today. The gardener found her here this morning, and she looked so pretty under the apple trees that we were delighted to have her stay a little while."

Ginny felt half-choked with a crazy mixture of rage and relief. She jammed her hands deep into her pockets and took a long, deep, shuddering breath. "We've been a little worried about her," she managed to say at last. "We didn't know where she was."

The woman waved her hands in a helpless gesture. "My husband and I have just recently moved here from the city and we believed this visit from your pony was one of the perfectly charming things that happen in the country."

Ginny decided quickly that it was safer for her not to try to say anything more. She hurried to her pony. Mokey raised her head from the green apples she had been eating on the ground and slobbered apple juice cheerfully down the front of Ginny's shirt. Ginny flung her arms around the pony's neck and wept briefly and thankfully into her mane.

Of course she had not thought, this time, to bring the bridle. For one moment she had a flash of panic, thinking she might have to leave Mokey here, which seemed unbearable, even for just a few minutes, now that she had found her at last. But then she thought to tug her belt from her blue jeans and loop it around Mokey's neck, just behind her ears. She led her triumphantly through the narrow gate.

"We would love to have her come visit us again," the young woman called to Ginny.

"Thank you, that would be very nice," Ginny managed to say, feeling a little kinder now that she had Mokey safely by her side. After all, she told herself firmly, if these people had never lived outside a city before, they might well believe that ponies wandered loose in orchards all the time. Ginny even found herself smiling. Mokey must have enjoyed being admired like a fine painting.

It was wonderful to have her safely home again. The police were notified and thanked, and Ginny sponged Mokey off with warm water. She was sweaty and covered with fly bites. The pony's usual cheerful disposition had turned quite sour by the time Ginny stopped fussing over her and shut her firmly in the stall. Ginny was sure this was due to too many hours in the heat and flies, so she gave the pony a full bucket of fresh cool water, which she drank thirstily, and then her evening feed of grain and hay, which did not seem to interest her very much. Then Ginny left her alone.

It was over. Ginny felt as limp as a soapy sponge. Her mother and father were as tired and relieved as she was, and dinner became a happy celebration.

"Your father and I had planned to go to the movies tonight," Mrs. Anderson said after the dishes were done. "Would you like to come with us?"

Ginny shook her head wearily. "No, thanks. I am going to take a bath, wash my hair, and not move again until morning!"

It was after ten o'clock when she finished brushing her hair dry and was ready for bed. In her bathrobe and slippers, happy and half-asleep, she went to say a last good night to her pony.

She turned on the garage light and went over to the stall, a lump of sugar in her hand. When she leaned over the door she caught her breath and let it out in a gasp. Mokey was standing in the middle of the stall with her head stuck out straight in front of her, her nostrils flaring as though she had been running. Her ears were back, her eyes were staring, her stomach was enormously swollen; and sweat dripped from her shoulders and sides. She was having trouble breathing and was obviously in great pain.

Ginny flew to the telephone to call for help and then stood, for a long, agonizing moment, trying to decide whom she should call. Her mother and father couldn't be reached, Michael was away—suddenly she remembered the veterinarian who had cared for their cat last summer when it had cut its paw. She couldn't remember his name. She hoped wildly that his number would be listed in her mother's book of special numbers. Veterinarian—Dr. Nichols. With shaking fingers, she dialed the number.

To her enormous relief, it was the doctor himself who answered the telephone. "Oh, please," Ginny gasped, "there's something terrible the matter with my pony, my parents aren't home, and I don't know what to do!"

In a quiet, steadying voice the doctor asked

a few questions, got Ginny's name and address, and then said, "Don't move the pony. Take away any feed or water from the stall, then let her absolutely alone. I'll be there in fifteen minutes."

Ginny hung up and tore back to the stall. Mokey always finished her oats, so she was sure the feed tub would be empty; she was astonished to find it was not. She unclipped the hooks and set the feed tub outside the stall, checked the water bucket and found it completely empty, and then shut the stall door. She glanced at her watch, frantic for something else to do. She realized suddenly that she was still in her bathrobe and slippers. She rushed upstairs, dressed, and rushed down again to turn on all the outside lights so that the veterinarian could find the house more easily.

A few minutes later she saw headlights coming down the drive. Without a wasted moment, the doctor lifted his black bag from the front seat of the car and followed Ginny to the pony's stall.

One quick glance at the suffering pony was all he needed. "What did she get into?" he asked sharply, a small bottle and a hypodermic syringe already in his hand. "Grain? Bran? Corn?"

79

Ginny stared at him blankly. "Oh!" she cried suddenly with a flash of understanding. "Apples! It must be the apples! She's been eating apples in an orchard all day long!"

"Put her halter on," Dr. Nichols said briefly. Ginny snatched the halter from its hook, then slipped it gently over the pony's head. The syringe was filled by now and the needle bit into the pony's neck. Mokey never moved. A second shot from another vial followed the first.

The doctor went on working over the gasping pony, the silence broken only when he spoke to Mokey in a low, reassuring voice. Finally he folded his stethoscope, took a deep breath, and left the stall. "Now we wait," he said. "And this is the hardest part of all. Twenty minutes." He checked the time on his watch.

"You aren't going to leave?" asked Ginny in a shaky voice.

"Of course not." He sat on a bale of hay and turned so that he could watch the motionless pony. "Now tell me what happened," he suggested.

He shook his head when Ginny had finished the story of this long and frantic day. "Apples," he said, "can be especially bad, because they ferment when they get into the stomach. But too much grain—or even too much grass, if the pony isn't used to it—can be just as dangerous. Horses and ponies can kill themselves by overeating; most other animals have more sense. I like horses, and I've owned and cared for them all my life, but they certainly seem to go out of their way to get themselves into trouble."

Ginny nodded vigorously. "But I've eaten too many apples," she said. "I've gotten a stomach ache sometimes, and once they made me sick, but Mokey looks—" she stopped and caught her breath "—she looks as though she might even die."

The doctor did not disagree with her, as Ginny had hoped he would. "She has a pretty bad case of colic," he said finally. "Horses and ponies can't vomit like dogs, or cats, or people. That's why your pony is in so much trouble. All those apples, and probably a bucket of water on top of them—" Ginny nodded miserably. "Her stomach is so swollen that we can only hope it doesn't burst before the medicine has time to work."

"If it bursts, she will die," Ginny said flatly.

"That's right. I really am sorry to have to tell you all this, but I want you to be prepared, just in case. It's a good thing you called me as quickly as you did."

He checked his watch, got up, gave Mokey two more shots and then another dose of medicine. The sweet, sharp smell filled the garage. Ginny peeked nervously at the pony in the stall. "She's not sweating so much," she said hopefully.

"That's only because I've given her something to relieve the pain," said the doctor. "This kind of thing is agony. At least she's not hurting so much now."

He stood for a moment, watching with concern as the pony struggled to breathe. "If there were a large animal hospital nearby, or a university with a veterinary school that had an operating room for horses, we might be able to get her there and operate in time. But the nearest one is several hundred miles from here, and in the condition she's in, the trip alone would probably kill her."

They waited in silence. A moth fluttered nervously around the lightbulb in the ceiling. Outside the garage door the crickets and locusts were making cheerful night noises, but inside there

was a strange quiet. Ginny realized, finally, that she was missing the sound of Mokey moving around in her stall, crunching her hay, and rattling her feed tub hopefully every once in a while.

The doctor rose to his feet and checked the pony again with his stethoscope. For the first time that night, he smiled. More shots. More medicine. Then he nodded reassuringly to Ginny. "Progress," he reported. "I really think she's going to make it, after all."

The hours went by in a gray haze. Ginny's mother and father came back from the movies, there were explanations, and coffee to make, and brief, anxious questions about the suffering pony.

Dawn came. The sun rose. At seven o'clock, Dr. Nichols checked the pony again. By this time, Mokey was poking her muzzle cheerfully into every corner of her stall, looking for a stray wisp of hay or one tiny spilled grain of oats to eat. Her stomach was back to normal size. Except for a light gray film of dried sweat on her sides and shoulders there was not a sign that there had been anything the matter with her at all.

"I'll just bet," said Ginny wearily, "that she'd eat all those apples again, right now!"

"She certainly would," agreed the doctor. "A lot of caring for horses and ponies is protecting them from their own foolishness." He snapped the clasp shut on his black bag. "You can give her two swallows of warmed water every hour, but absolutely *nothing* to eat. I'll be back this evening after office hours to check her again." He rumpled Mokey's black forelock, looking, Ginny thought, almost as tired, and just as glad, as she felt herself.

"To bed with you, young lady," her mother said firmly to Ginny as the doctor drove away. "I am perfectly capable of giving that pony of yours two swallows of water—yes, I know, warmed— once every hour."

Still protesting that she wanted to take care of Mokey herself, Ginny stumbled up the stairs and barely managed to kick her sneakers off before throwing herself on her bed and falling asleep.

Chapter Eight

Ginny stood by the gate to the white-fenced show ring. Gay marching music came from the loudspeakers; the red and white flags marking the outside course snapped in the brisk early morning breeze. Ponies of all sizes and shapes whirled in circling patterns all across the vivid green of the polo field where the show was being held.

The music stopped and the announcer's low, clear voice sounded across the field, calling the first class of the day.

"Model ponies, large division. Bring your ponies to the ring, please."

Ginny backed away as the wide gate swung open and a crowd of gleaming ponies surged into the ring, all of them without saddles, led by their riders on foot. This class was to be judged only on the ponies' looks. Pam was in the ring with her coppery Firefly who was dancing, as usual, at the end of his reins; there were bays and blacks and browns and grays, but no spots, Ginny noticed. All the ponies had their manes done up in small braids and the tops of their tails were braided, as well.

Ginny shivered with excitement. Pam had finally persuaded her to enter Mokey in this show and the pony was waiting in Pam's trailer in the shade of the huge old oaks on the edge of the polo field. Michael had spent the past week teaching Ginny how to shorten and thin out the pony's mane and then do it up properly in braids.

It took a lot of practice, Ginny found. The first five or six times she'd tried it the mane wasn't short enough and the braids were limp and lumpy. Finally, though, even Michael had to nod his approval.

The braiding of the tail had been a different matter. Remembering, Ginny made a face. She understood how it was done, but no matter how tightly she pulled the first few strands at the top of the tail, no matter how nice it looked when it was finished, the moment Mokey switched her tail at a fly, the whole thing started unraveling. Ginny tried so many times that even Mokey became impatient, and Michael finally came to the rescue and told her to let it be, that he would do it for her the morning of the show.

Now Mokey was waiting for her first class, mane done up, smartly braided tail (courtesy of Michael) snugly wrapped in a protective bandage, while Ginny stood by the ring and watched Pam's first class.

The two judges were walking slowly around each pony, standing back to get an overall picture, moving on to the next, then separating them into two lines.

Firefly was standing perfectly with his weight

properly balanced on all four legs, his red-gold coat shimmering in the sunlight and his small ears pricked toward Pam.

The winners were announced and a pewter-gray pony with a snow-white mane and tail left the ring with the blue ribbon fluttering from his bridle, a rather unpleasant look of triumph on his owner's face. Pam held Firefly back to let the gray go through the gate, then followed him out and handed Firefly's reins, and the second-place red ribbon, to Michael.

"Very nice, Miss Pam," said Michael, throwing a wide light wool blanket over the chestnut pony. "We'll just get this cooler on you, young fellow. The breeze is still a bit fresh this time of day." Whistling cheerfully, he led the pony back toward the trailer. Pam came over to join Ginny at the ring fence.

"That gray is a perfectly lovely pony," Pam said with enthusiasm. "He's an English Anglo-Arab—half Thoroughbred and half Arabian. This is the first time I've seen him. He's only been in this country about six weeks."

Pam glanced at her watch. "Your first class is coming up in half an hour. You'd better get Mokey."

Ginny stomped along beside Pam on the way over to the trailer. Her new jodhpur boots felt stiff and heavy, her jodhpur breeches felt strange, and she was sure she was slowly strangling in her long-sleeved shirt with its tight collar and tie.

She struggled into her new blue riding coat when they reached the trailer, crammed her hard black hunt cap on top of her head, and surveyed Mokey gloomily. "*You*," she whispered crossly to Mokey, "are pretending to be something you are *not*. I have never seen so many glorious ponies in one place in my entire life, and I can't imagine what we are doing here." Mokey helped herself to another mouthful of hay from the rope net tied high in front of her, sneezed, and went on eating.

Michael put Firefly into the adjoining stall of the trailer and backed Mokey carefully down the ramp. He slipped her bridle on, over Ginny's protests—"Honestly, Michael, don't bother, I can do that myself!"—and settled the saddle onto Mokey's back.

"She looks sort of strange," said Ginny doubtfully. Pam laughed. "You're just not used to seeing her all braided up and with a saddle on her," she said. "But you can't very well ride her bareback today! Just be glad we were able to borrow one that fit her."

Michael gestured to Ginny. "Give you a leg up for luck," he said, swinging Ginny up into the saddle. Ginny groped for her stirrups, decided they were too long, shortened them, then changed her mind and let them down again. She had practiced with Mokey for several days with the borrowed saddle, but it still felt strange after having ridden the pony bareback for so long.

Mokey stood patiently while Ginny fiddled about with her stirrups and reins. Michael unwrapped the tail bandage, checked the tightness of the girth, and went over the pony one more time with a soft linen cloth.

"Bring your ponies to the ring gate," the loudspeaker called, "for Class Eleven, Pony Working Hunters, over the outside course."

"Now, remember," said Pam, walking beside Mokey, "the looks of the ponies do not count in this class. They are judged only on their manners and their performance over the outside course, and on the way they move and jump."

"Okay," said Ginny. Then, faintly, "I think I am going to be sick to my stomach."

"No, you're not," said Pam firmly. "Take deep

breaths. We'll get your number listed and find out how soon your turn is, then you'd better get busy warming up."

"Okay," whispered Ginny. After Pam checked in at the gate and found Mokey would be the seventh to go on the course, Ginny trotted Mokey far out on the polo field. She began to feel much better once she was alone on her pony, trotting and cantering in wide circles on the smooth grass.

She caught sight of Pam waving to her, much too soon. Regretfully, she turned Mokey back toward the ring.

"You're next," said Pam.

"Yuk," said Ginny.

Pam stepped back with a sympathetic grin. The wide white gate swung open and Mokey walked into the ring.

Ginny was numb with nervousness. Somehow she managed to gather her reins into a short tangle and push Mokey into a canter. She circled toward the first jump. Mokey raised her head and pricked her ears.

"Oh, gosh," wailed Pam to Michael. "I never thought! I'll bet Mokey has never seen a brush fence in her life!"

Mokey never had seen such a thing; neither had Ginny. It was nothing more than short evergreen branches packed tightly into a long white wooden stand, but it looked hairy and enormous, and Mokey faltered uncertainly. Ginny sat unmoving in the saddle, completely forgetting everything she had practiced so hard, so many times, in the schooling field. The bewildered pony slowed to a trot.

Ginny became vaguely aware that things were not right. From some dim working corner of her mind she managed to remember to give Mokey an encouraging kick and then grab hold of the braided mane. Reassured that she really was supposed to jump that strange green thing in front of her, Mokey trotted forward and jumped the brush with an enormous spring that tossed Ginny, gasping, up onto her neck and then back with a jolt into the saddle.

Mokey landed and cantered on. Ginny poked her feet back into the stirrups, tipped her cap back where it belonged, and generally gathered herself together before they came to the next fence, which was a very comfortable-looking stone wall of a size and type they had jumped many times before this.

Mokey jumped it well. The course swung to the left between two flags. Ginny began riding her pony instead of merely sitting in a helpless lump, and they began to enjoy themselves. Over a gate, neatly through an in-and-out, and then a zigzag rail fence; two more fences, and then they finished the course over a last brush fence, the twin of the first, which led back into the ring. Mokey jumped this with effortless ease, and even bobbed her head and gave a flip of her tail as she landed, obviously pleased with herself and her performance. Her face glowing with delight, Ginny pulled up and trotted from the ring.

"Wasn't she wonderful?" she gasped, flinging herself out of the saddle and giving Mokey a hug. Pam and Michael joined in warm congratulations. The unfortunate first jump was mentioned only indirectly, as Mokey was being sponged off and walked in the shade.

"You'll be all right from now on, Miss Ginny," Michael said kindly. "There can't ever be another first fence in your first class in your first show."

"Thank goodness for that," said Ginny feelingly.

Chapter Nine

The show went on through the morning. Pam won a big class with Firefly over the outside course, and then another in the ring. The beautiful gray pony, whose name, they discovered in the program, was Ashes, did not jump very well in his hunter class. "He's young and still very inexperienced," explained Pam. But he went very well in the walk, trot, and canter class in the ring, and he and Firefly were chosen to work together for several minutes before the judges' decision went to Pam's pony.

It was obvious that the girl on the gray pony was not at all pleased with the way things were going. In one brief moment, when the judges were not looking, she let her pony barge up against Firefly. There was an instant of confusion. The girl on the gray apologized sweetly to Pam, who smiled back politely, but then moved Firefly to the far side of the ring. The chestnut pony was upset, Ginny noticed with a sinking heart. She could see the white showing around his eyes and his ears were flicking back and forth as they always did when he was nervous. Although Ginny thought that Pam was probably angry, she noticed that Pam's expression remained calm and unruffled. She spoke softly to her pony and soon had him settled down.

"What was that all about?" asked Ginny after the class was over. "Was all that fuss on purpose, or was it an accident? It was hard to tell."

Pam's mouth set briefly into a grim line. "That

97

Angela Longworth is a pain," she said. "Firefly hates feeling crowded, and she knows it. But that new pony of hers is too nice to need that kind of foolishness; he's good enough on his own."

Watching the two girls ride in a later class, Ginny thought how easy they made it look. The two glorious ponies moved like precision clocks with hardly a waste motion by either pony or rider. "This Angela person may be a pill," Ginny commented to Mokey later, "but she sure can ride." Firefly shied and played in this class, and had to be content with a white ribbon for fourth place while the gray pony was first.

At the lunch break the two girls sprawled in the shade with a picnic basket, their coats off and their collars open.

"You know, Ginny," Pam said at last after several awkward starts, "I really am sorry I talked you into bringing Mokey to this show."

"Whatever for?" gasped Ginny, sitting up in surprise.

"I don't think it was fair to start you off with such fierce competition," answered Pam. "It seems as though every good show pony in the country is here today. This particular show used to be small and friendly and fun, and I guess I was remembering how it used to be when I persuaded you to come with me today."

"Never mind," said Ginny, flopping down in the grass again. "Mokey is very special, but this is all a bit over her head. Don't worry about it, though. It's fun to be part of all this—" she waved her sandwich at the polo field and the white-fenced ring. "Anyway, we only entered her in two classes. We never did plan to make a big thing of this." She took a bite of sandwich and mumbled around the edges. "Stop worrying and save your energy for beating that ghastly Angela. You'll need it."

"But," Ginny said quietly to Mokey later as she went to put her bridle on for the next class, "it sure would be fun to win a ribbon." She sighed, patted Mokey apologetically, and backed her out of the trailer.

Firefly whinnied frantically as Ginny led Mokey away. Michael was at the pony's head in a moment, calming him down. Ginny saddled Mokey and trotted off to warm up, promising herself that this time she would keep her wits about her and not let herself get so nervous that she forgot how to ride.

She nearly managed to keep calm. Everything went well until the very last moment when, waiting to go into the ring, she heard a shout from Michael and a shriek from Pam. She pulled Mokey out of line, wondering fearfully what she had done. "Hey, wait, Mokey's still got the bandage on her tail!" cried Pam. Flustered and annoyed with herself, Ginny felt her face growing red as Pam took hold of Mokey's bridle to hold her still while Michael swiftly unwound the bandage.

"Okay now," said Pam with a giggle. "She'd have looked a little funny going around the course with that still on."

"Gosh," said Ginny, furious with herself. "There's so darned much to remember."

"Never you mind," Michael spoke quietly. "You just get in there with that good pony and give her a chance to show what she can do."

"Right," Ginny said firmly. She gathered her reins smoothly and deliberately and rode Mokey in through the open gate.

Mokey went well, from the first green brush to

the last. Ginny was quietly very pleased as she trotted out of the ring. Michael was pleased, too. She could tell by his wordless nod as he reached for Mokey's reins. "Thanks, Michael, but I'll cool her out," said Ginny as she slid from the saddle. "Her halter is in the trailer, isn't it?"

"I wouldn't untack her just yet," said Michael. "Loosen her girth and walk her around. You might be wanted back in the ring after a round like that."

A surge of hope swept over Ginny. "You mean we might get a ribbon?" she said weakly.

"Not necessarily," cautioned Michael. "There are only four ribbons, but the judges will call about ten ponies back, and from what I have seen of the others in this class so far, Mokey just might be one of them."

"Oh, wow," said Ginny. She walked Mokey for a few minutes and then Michael began rubbing the pony down. Mokey, who wanted to eat the short, sweet grass of the polo field and was forbidden to do so because her bit would get stained, looked bored. The last pony finished the course, there was a pause of several minutes, then the loudspeaker called: "Bring the following ponies into the ring, please." Mokey's number was the fourth to be called.

"Quick, tell me what to do now," Ginny said frantically.

"Just get on and ride her in," said Pam. "The ringmaster will tell you what to do."

They were asked to line up in single file in the order their numbers had been called. The judges held a brief consultation, checked the numbers on their cards, and then the ringmaster in his scarlet coat came over to Ginny, touched his top hat, and requested that she and the girl on the bay in line in front of her change places.

This moved Mokey up to third place in line. Ginny felt she could not survive one more moment of suspense. She managed to keep Mokey standing well and tried to look knowledgeable and efficient.

Finally one of the judges waved his card and the first pony trotted across the ring. A chestnut followed, and then Ginny on Mokey. Three or four others were called. Ginny knew all of them were being trotted out for soundness; the judges were looking to see if any of the ponies were lame, because a lame pony could not be awarded a ribbon. She knew she had nothing to worry about—Mokey was perfectly sound.

Another pause. The judges spoke to the ringmaster, who went to the announcer's stand. Mokey was tired; Ginny could feel her sigh and start to droop a little. Some riders were dismounting and holding their ponies to rest them; Ginny did the same. She saw Michael nod his approval from the side of the ring. The loudspeaker crackled briefly. The show veterinarian was being called.

He came into the ring, spoke to the judges, then walked along the line of waiting ponies, looking them over with swift, professional care, not touching them and not paying any more attention to one than to another.

The ponies were then asked to jog again. This time Ginny led Mokey at a trot, as most of the others were doing. It must have been hot; later, Ginny was to find her shirt soaking wet under her coat, and her hair, under the black hunt cap, as wet as though she had been in a shower. But she did not notice now.

The vet wrote something on each of the judges' cards, shook hands with them, and left the ring.

The judges signed their cards, handed them to the ringmaster, and walked across to the judges' stand.

Time stood still. Ginny could hear two other riders whispering, wondering which pony had been questioned. The girl with the bright bay pony who was now fourth in line, behind Mokey, joined them and Ginny heard her laugh and say, "I just know they called the vet to look at that spotted thing. You can tell it's blind in one eye and the rules say that is an unsoundness."

Ginny felt her face flushing with anger. Mokey was not blind, just because her eyes did not match! She fought to keep her expression as calm and dignified as she could. Wouldn't the judges know? Certainly the vet could tell, couldn't he? After all of this awful waiting, could they take Mokey's ribbon away just because she had one blue eye and one brown?

At last the announcer's voice came over the loudspeakers. "We have the results of Class Twelve, Pony Working Hunters—"

The blue ribbon and a silver plate were won by a boy on a seal brown pony. The red ribbon went to a blaze-faced chestnut, and then the ringmaster was tipping his hat to Ginny and pinning the golden yellow ribbon for third place on Mokey's bridle.

Ginny never knew who was fourth. She never remembered leaving the ring. Michael's usually stern face was wreathed in smiles. "Very nice, Miss Ginny," he said. Pam was speechless with delight. She hugged Mokey fiercely and found her voice at last. "Terrific," she said.

They led Mokey to the trailer with the yellow ribbon fluttering on her bridle. With quiet pleasure all three helped to take the saddle and bridle off the tired pony and put on her halter. Ginny held her in silence while Michael sponged her off. When he was done, he reached for the lead rope, but Ginny shook her head. "Please," she said. "Let me take her." She put the yellow ribbon in her pocket and led Mokey away from the crowds and the ring toward the far edge of the polo field, where the grass grew long under the trees.

She sat down and leaned back against a tree trunk while Mokey cropped the grass quietly at the end of the lead rope. The late afternoon sun slanted across the field, throwing long shadows and blazing in the tops of the trees. Ginny took

the ribbon out of her pocket and smoothed it on one knee. In a weary haze of happiness she put her head back and squinted through her lashes up at the patterns of leaves above her.

Suddenly Ginny sat up and then scrambled to her feet. The yellow ribbon, which had meant so much just a moment before, fell, unnoticed, into the grass as she looked at the branches above her.

There. She had seen it again. She couldn't imagine why she hadn't noticed before. There was a patch of red-gold leaves just over her head.

Slowly she found the ribbon, stuffed it into her pocket, and went over to Mokey. It wasn't just the late sunlight that was setting the trees on fire. The leaves were starting to turn. Summer was almost over.

Chapter Ten

"Of course it is all quite impossible." Mr. Anderson tapped his pipe firmly in his hand. "We have no place to keep a pony in the winter, even if we could afford to buy her, which I very much doubt."

"I know," Ginny said helplessly. She and her

father leaned on the top rail of the paddock and watched Mokey shaking the seeds out of her hay so she could eat them separately.

Ginny giggled suddenly. "There was a gray pony at the show last weekend that cost eighteen thousand dollars."

Mr. Anderson turned to stare at Ginny in disbelief. "Now, young lady, that simply can't be true."

Ginny was positive. "Everybody at the show was talking about it. It was a beautiful pony."

"I should hope so!" said Mr. Anderson. "And I suppose your wonderful Mokey beat it in the hunter class?"

Ginny giggled again. "That would be something, wouldn't it! But they weren't even in the same classes."

"Probably just as well," said her father. "It wouldn't do at all to have a rented summer pony beat eighteen thousand dollars on the hoof."

"Handsome is as handsome does," said Ginny firmly.

"Quite right."

Mokey wandered over to the paddock fence and gazed longingly at the grass out of her reach.

She pushed with annoyance at the rails which barred her way. But each rail in the entire paddock had been nailed firmly into place the day after she had escaped and found the apple orchard, and she could not push them down. With a bored sigh, she turned back to her hay.

Ginny and her father walked in silence to the house. They had had this conversation several times before. Mokey did not belong to them. She belonged to Mr. Dobbs and the ghastly Sweetbriar Pony Farm, she had been rented only for the summer, and there was nothing, absolutely nothing, Ginny could do.

She had thought wildly of so many answers through so many sleepless nights, all of them either crazy or impractical, which amounted to the same thing. She'd even thought of asking Pam if her father would buy Mokey, but then she had met Mr. Jennings one day. He was tall and forbidding and stern, and did not look at all like the kind of person who would allow a rather strangely spotted pony with unmatching eyes in his stable full of beautiful horses.

Ginny finished cleaning Mokey's stall and dumped the wheelbarrow down by the garden.

She had the pony bedded on peat moss now, which Mokey would not eat as she had her straw bedding. This was much better for her, and Mr. Anderson was pleased because the peat moss was good for his treasured vegetable garden.

Tired of worrying, tired of not being able to find an answer, Ginny rattled the wheelbarrow angrily back to the garage and took the bridle off the hook. At least she could still ride, and this always made her feel better.

But, by now, there were too many reminders that summer was over. The trees were all changing colors and, in the open fields, the grass was drying to a soft russet red.

Though Ginny spent the whole afternoon on Mokey's back, it had not helped very much, and she finally turned toward home, knowing she was being silly and unreasonable, knowing her mother and father felt almost as bad as she did, and promising herself not to make things any more difficult or unhappy than they already were.

Feeling older and wiser and pleased with her decision, she jogged down the driveway and then pulled up with a jerk that brought the surprised pony to a sliding stop. Mr. Dobbs's battered

green pickup truck was standing by the garage.

Ginny whirled Mokey around and kicked her into a gallop. Small stones scattered wildly from the pony's flying hoofs. They crossed the road and Ginny pressed her pony on deeper into the darkening woods.

There was a fallen log across the path which Ginny and Pam had jumped several times through the summer. It was old and streaked with moss and almost impossible to see in the failing evening light. Mokey was galloping too fast to check herself when the log loomed out of the shadows. She hit it with her knees and turned over.

Ginny opened her eyes and blinked with surprise. It was almost dark, and blurry stars were shining in little patches through the wavering branches of the trees. She was on her back in the ferns and dead leaves beside the path and her head ached fiercely.

She sat up slowly, but the woods spun and tilted around her, making her so dizzy she had to lie down again. The crushed ferns smelled good. She closed her eyes.

She felt a warm breath down the side of her

neck. It was Mokey, pushing at Ginny with her muzzle. "Hi, Moke." Ginny struggled to sit up again. Vaguely, she noticed the reins were broken and trailing in uneven lengths from the pony's bit. She held onto a tree and swayed to her feet, clutching at Mokey's mane to keep her balance. "I think we've got some kind of a problem," she said in an uneven voice. "I've broken the bridle that doesn't even belong to me." It seemed a great problem and Ginny stood dizzily by her pony, worrying. "The only thing to do is go home now, I guess, and tell Pam." She turned her aching head slowly. Mokey's back looked a long way up.

Ginny could never remember later how she finally managed to get on Mokey's back, pick up the broken reins, and turn toward home. The pony walked slowly. Ginny sang a little to herself, but this made her head ache more, so she went back to worrying about the broken bridle again.

There were lights on everywhere when she got home. Her head was clearing slightly and, in the floodlights outside the garage, she dimly recognized Michael up on one of Mr. Jennings's big hunters, and Pam, white-faced, trying to calm her frantic Firefly. "We can't find her anywhere," she heard Pam say, and then Mokey whinnied a loud greeting to Firefly.

"Hi," said Ginny, suddenly feeling very foolish. "I broke your bridle."

There were cries of relief and suddenly people were holding Mokey, helping Ginny down. Though her knees felt very peculiar when she walked, Ginny insisted on leading Mokey into the lights by the garage to make sure the pony wasn't hurt. "I really did it this time," Ginny said to Michael. "I jumped alone, and I jumped without my hard hat, and I don't think I will ever do it again."

"I believe that is very true," answered Michael, and said nothing more. Ginny realized, gratefully, that he would never mention it again.

Feeling vague and confused, Ginny leaned against her father's arm. "Whatever happened to Mr. Dobbs?" she asked finally. "Did he give up and go away?" Then she grinned at Mokey. "If he did, it was worth it," she said.

Mrs. Anderson came up beside her. "For two cents I'd send that pony right back where she came from!" she said in a shaking voice. "Ginny, what an unbelievably stupid thing to do! Mr. Dobbs was here because your father and I asked him to come. We wanted to find out, at least, how much he might want for Mokey."

"Oh," said Ginny. She blinked up at the lights over the garage. There seemed to her to be two lights wherever there should be just one.

"There was talk of the humane society closing his place down," said Mr. Anderson. "But now that won't be necessary. A supermarket chain has bought his land for a great deal of money and he is selling off his ponies just as quickly as he can. It is extremely fortunate for us, because he must get rid of them. He offered us Mokey for very little more than we've already paid to rent her."

He stopped for a moment and shook his head. "He didn't seem to think she was worth very much, but then he hasn't seen what you've done with her this summer."

"You mean that Mokey is mine?" said Ginny.

"Yes."

"And she can stay here always?"

"That's right."

"In the garage?"

"No. We've decided to keep our car for another

year instead of buying a new one. We'll use the money to build a small stable down near the paddock instead."

"And so I fell on my head, and practically broke Mokey's neck, for absolutely no reason at all."

She leaned her aching head against Mokey's warm shoulder and was surprised to feel tears sliding down her cheeks. Mrs. Anderson quietly vanished into the house to call the doctor and turn down Ginny's bed. Pam and Michael murmured a smiling "good night" and rode off into the dark. Wordlessly, Ginny looked up at her father.

"It's been quite a summer," he said.

Together, they put Mokey away in her stall. The pony rattled her feed tub demandingly. She was making it quite clear, thought Ginny, that there had been enough emotional fussing for one day. It was late, it was long past suppertime, and Mokey was hungry.

Chapter Eleven

Ginny was fidgeting in bed the next afternoon, bored and restless. She no longer was seeing double, but her head ached when she tried to read.

There was a light knock on her door and Pam came in, holding an apple in one hand as she had the first time they had met early in the summer. It seemed so long ago.

"Hi!" Pam pulled up a chair and sat down by the bed. "You look pale and perfectly awful, just like your mother said you did. How do you feel?"

Ginny grinned. "Fine," she said. "I'm very glad you came. I've got nothing to do but feel foolish, and I'm tired of that."

"Michael and my father and mother all send their best wishes," announced Pam. She bit into the apple. "This is for Mokey, actually, not for you," she explained. "And I'm sure she won't mind if I have a little. Your mother said you couldn't eat an apple, anyway."

"Nothing but tea and toast and hot nourishing soup," said Ginny. "Yuk."

"My father says," Pam went on, "that since you have given yourself a royal concussion, he hopes you've knocked some sense into your head, because even Mokey can't jump in the dark."

Ginny stared at her. "*Even* Mokey?"

"Even Mokey." Pam nodded dramatically. "He says that Mokey has more sense than the two of us put together, and that he is one of her greatest admirers, and would you do us the favor of letting

119

us take care of her for you until you can do it again yourself."

"You're kidding." Ginny shook her head but then stopped quickly because it made her dizzy. "You mean, in your stable, with Firefly, and all those beautiful horses?"

"That's right. And Michael says he will let me help." Pam grinned. "I never was very interested in caring for horses and ponies, and Michael had about given me up as hopeless. But you've had so much fun with Mokey, and taking care of her seems to be such a nice part of it, that I feel I've missed a lot."

Ginny sat up straighter in bed and clasped her arms around her knees. "The doctor said I can't ride for at least four more weeks. Will you exercise her every single day, even after school starts?"

"Oh, sure," said Pam. "That will be the nicest part of all."

Ginny stared at her friend. "You mean you've wanted to ride Mokey before this?" she asked.

"For ages."

Ginny leaned her head back against the pillows. The room was tilting a little bit around the edges. "Thank your father very much," she said. "Mokey would love to visit. But will you be sure to tell Michael that she gets three quarts of mixed crushed oats and sweet feed, morning and night, and that she should have a little grass every day, and that she's terribly fussy about her water being clean . . ." She stopped and laughed at herself. "Okay, I guess he knows how."

Pam smiled understandingly. "I'll tell him," she promised.

Ginny stood by the window of her room and watched Pam ride Mokey down the driveway. The pony was striding along cheerfully, as she always did, and Ginny saw Pam lean forward and pat the pony fondly on the shoulder. Ginny sighed enviously.

A light breeze sprang up and a shower of yellow leaves spun down from the maple tree on the lawn. The afternoon smelled of sunlight and falling leaves and there was even a slight hint of frost in the air.

Ginny smiled to herself as she went back to bed. Her father was right. It had been quite a summer.